CW00968429

# Gordon Gets
# EVEN

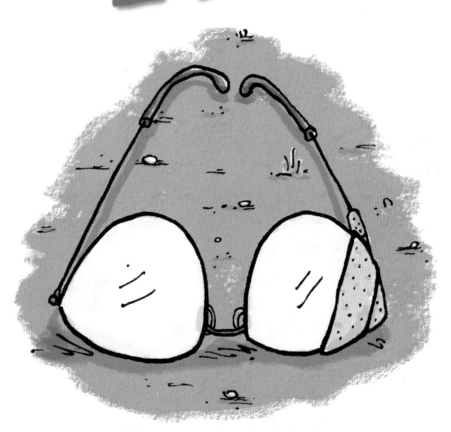

Written by Linda Strachan

Illustrated by Kelly Waldek

# Chapter 1

"You've all seen the graffiti on the wall of the new gym hall." The head teacher scanned the room. "Someone must know who did it. I really don't want to have to involve the police at this stage, so I would like that someone to come and talk to me."

Gordon pretended to look around the hall, like everyone else. The only person he didn't look at was Big Kev.

"Who do you think did it?" asked Ranjit, Gordon's best friend.

Gordon shrugged. "Dunno."

At lunch time Big Kev was waiting. He wasn't much taller than Gordon but he was mean and had a vicious streak. He grabbed Gordon by the collar and pushed him against the wall, knocking Gordon's glasses to the ground.

"You tell anyone what you saw and you're for it, Gogs."

"I… I won't, Kev. Honest, I won't."

"You'd better not. I'll have my eye on you and if I think you've squealed, I'll sort you out."

"Gordon, come on we need a goalie!" Ranjit shouted.

Big Kev let him go with a scowl. Gordon retrieved his glasses and made a dash for freedom.

"We're expecting some special visitors shortly," said Mrs Harper that afternoon.

Everyone looked excited. Gordon tried to sit so low in his chair that he was almost under his desk.

"Who are they?" asked Sarah Goodie.

"The Police are coming to talk about how to look after yourself when you're out and about."

"How many policemen are coming?" asked Ranjit. Gordon glared at him.

"I don't know," said Mrs Harper. "We'll find out when they get here."

"Gordon, would you go to the school office and escort our visitors to the classroom?"

Gordon shrank further down into his seat. He looked pleadingly at Mrs Harper but she just smiled.

7

Gordon moved like a snail over to the classroom door. He clumped slowly down the stairs and through the empty hall. He dawdled for ages at the office door but a teacher came along and frowned at him, so finally he knocked.

"Hello, Gordon," said a policewoman as the door to the office opened.

Gordon looked at his feet.

"Oh!" said the school secretary. "Do you know WPC Potts, Gordon?"

The policewoman grinned. "Gordon is my nephew."

Gordon didn't grin back as he led his aunt towards the classroom. What if Big Kev saw him with a policewoman?

Just as that thought entered Gordon's head, Big Kev came around the corner. Big Kev said nothing, but his hard stare told Gordon he would be in big trouble later. Gordon barely heard what Aunt Caroline had to say, but he remembered thinking that it wasn't only strangers who were dangerous.

Sure enough, Big Kev was waiting for Gordon after school.

"What've you been tellin' the Fuzz?"

"Nothing, Kev. Nothing at all. Honest. I didn't say a thing – I just showed her the way to the classroom."

Big Kev grabbed Gordon by the hair and pulled until his eyes began to water.

"Better not have said anything about that graffiti, or I'll get you, right?"

"Right," gasped Gordon, barely able to breathe. He wanted to be the kind of person that fought back, but he was too scared. He just wanted Big Kev to let him go.

"What's going on here?" demanded the school caretaker, who appeared as if from nowhere.

"Nothing." Big Kev let Gordon go. "We were just foolin' around, weren't we, Gogs?  Me an' Gogs are good pals." He put his hand on Gordon's shoulder, pinching hard so that Gordon couldn't run off.

"Away you go home, the two of you," the caretaker said. He watched them all the way to the corner of the street.

As soon as he could, Gordon squirmed away from Big Kev and ran all the way home. He hated being called Gogs and he hated Big Kev for being such a bully. But worst of all he hated himself because he felt so pathetic and helpless.

# Chapter 2

Gordon let himself in through the back door. He could hear voices in the living room. It was his mum and Aunt Caroline and they were talking about him.

"Gordon was acting very strangely at school today," Aunt Caroline was saying. "He seemed upset about something."

"Perhaps I should speak to his teacher," his mother said.

"No way!" Gordon thought. If Big Kev found out his mum had been speaking to Mrs Harper, he would beat him up for sure.

Gordon tiptoed through the hall and up to his room.
What was he going to do? Perhaps if he could have a word
with Aunt Caroline first, he could make her understand.

After tea Gordon managed to speak to his aunt, while his
mum was doing the washing up. He told her all about how
Big Kev had threatened and bullied him but he decided not
to tell her about the graffiti.

"I know Kevin Grintle," Aunt Caroline said. "He's a real troublemaker, but he's also a coward. Tell you what – I'm on duty near the school tomorrow with one of my colleagues, PC Derek Hopkins. What if we just happen to come along and see Kevin and you outside school? We could have a few words with him."

Gordon grinned. "That would be great! That way he would never know it was all arranged beforehand."

All the next day Gordon felt much more sure of himself. He was going to stand up to Big Kev – with a little help from Aunt Caroline. He even managed to stand tall as he approached Big Kev in the corridor. "Wait till after school," Big Kev snarled as he went past.

But when the final school bell went Gordon's confidence left him.

What if Aunt Caroline had forgotten? What if there was no one there to help him? He began to feel sick.

Big Kev was lurking at the end of the road. Gordon looked around but there was no sign of anyone in a police uniform. He walked as slowly as he could but still he couldn't see PC Hopkins or Aunt Caroline.

"Told you I'd be waiting for you," Big Kev growled.

Just before his glasses were knocked to the ground again, Gordon saw someone across the road. It looked like a police officer. Now was his chance to stand up to Big Kev.

"Just leave me alone, you big bully," Gordon cried. You know that policewoman in school? Well, that's my aunt and she says she knows all about you," Gordon said, in a loud voice. "And I haven't told her anything ... so ... you must have lots of other things to hide."

Big Kev just stared at him. To Gordon's surprise he looked worried. "Is she going to tell my dad?"

Gordon just shrugged. "Dunno. Hey, isn't that your dad over there?"

"I'm off!" Big Kev shouted as he turned and ran away.

Gordon was shaking, but he felt a warm glow inside. He picked up his glasses and looked around for the police officer. All he could see was a traffic warden standing by a car. There, coming round the corner were Aunt Caroline and PC Hopkins.

"I'm sorry, Gordon," said Aunt Caroline. "We were called away. Are you okay?"

"Yeah, I'm okay," said Gordon. "And I don't think Big Kev will be bothering me any more."